This Little Tiger book belongs to:

_____

_____

_____

For Annie, Eva, Dan and Dixie
~ D B

For Aaron and Isaac
~ P I

LITTLE TIGER PRESS
1 The Coda Centre, 189 Munster Road, London SW6 6AW
www.littletigerpress.com
First published in Great Britain 2001
This edition published 2012
by Little Tiger Press, London
Text copyright © David Bedford 2001
Illustrations copyright © Penny Ives 2001
David Bedford and Penny Ives have asserted their rights
to be identified as the author and illustrator of this work
under the Copyright, Designs and Patents Act, 1988
All rights reserved • ISBN 978-1-85430-747-7
Printed in China • LTP/1900/0453/0512
2 4 6 8 10 9 7 5 3 1

THE LONG JOURNEY HOME

David Bedford   Penny Ives

LITTLE TIGER PRESS

Dixie woke up. What was that noise?
There was something whimpering . . .

so he crept through the hole
in the fence to see who it was.

Behind the fence he found a kitten.
"I've lost my mother!" it wailed.

Dixie looked around. "Does she have a stripy tail?"
"Yes!" said the kitten. "And pointy ears."
"Follow me," said Dixie. "I'll take you to her."

"Thank you, Dixie!" said the
kitten's mother, but Dixie
didn't hear her because . . .

he'd already gone to see who was hopping
up and down among the long grasses.
Boing! Boing! Boing! it went.

"Why are you bouncing?"
asked Dixie.
    "I can't fly yet," said the
baby owl. "And I'm
looking for my mother."

Boing!

Boing!

Boing!

"Does she live in the trees?" asked Dixie.

"Yes she does," said the baby owl.

"Then follow me," he said.

Boing!

Boing!

Boing!

"Thank you, Dixie!" called the
owl's mother, but Dixie didn't hear.
He'd already gone further into the
woods to see who was making that
terrible noise.

YOW-WOW-WOW-WOWWWWWWWWWWWWwww

"*YOW!*" cried the fox cub. "I can't find my way home."

"Where do you live?" asked Dixie.

"In the side of a hill," said the fox cub.

"Follow me," said Dixie. "I can see your mother looking for you."

"Thank you, Dixie," said the fox
cub's mother. "But shouldn't you be
home by now? It'll soon be dark."
Dixie turned to go, but . . .

. . . which way was home?

Everything looked
different in the dark.

Dixie was lost.

"Don't worry," said the foxes, "we'll show you where to go."

They led Dixie to the edge of the woods.

"We don't know the way from here," said the cubs' mother.

Dixie didn't know the way either. What was he going to do next?

"Look, Dixie, I can fly now!" called
the baby owl. "Follow us!"
    Dixie followed the little owl and his
family through the moonlight, until
he came to the long grass.

"We don't know where to go from here," said the baby owl.

"But we do," squeaked a small voice. "Come with us."

Dixie followed the
kitten and his mother
through the tunnels
in the grass until . . .

he knew exactly where he was! There was
the hole in the fence, and there, on the
other side, someone was waiting for him.

"I've been looking for you everywhere!" said Dixie's mother. "You shouldn't have gone out on your own in the dark. You could have got lost."